I0756080

400 Ways to Say "I Love You"

Love Notes

by

Robin B. Roundtree

DOD Publications

The Flowered Robin

Dedication

Love is powerful, but finding the rights words to express it can be challenging!

A simple yet meaningful love note speaks volumes! It gives someone special a gift they will remember and appreciate for a lifetime.

Dedicated to those who love, love!

Love Notes

1. You're a birdsong at the break of day, on the dawn of Spring. Softly whistling as I pray, that's the kind of joy you bring.
2. Within your arms I love to rest, To me you'll always be the best.
3. I don't know which one is sweeter: honey, syrup, sugar, or you.
4. You get me, and I love that!
5. If sunshine burns, then every time you look at me, I'm on fire!
6. Just when I thought I could never love again, love began in you.
7. I STILL do!
8. Understand this: you are loved and adored beyond measure!
9. I love us. We just fit!
10. The love you show me comforts, assures, and brings peace to my soul. I can't express what that means to me. I love you so much!
11. I don't need expensive things when I have you. You're priceless!
12. You are clearly a gift from God!
13. I never believed that love would ever find me. Then I met you! Now never is forever.
14. One minute without you is way too long!
15. This love story is so good that the author retired.
16. What is the splendor of the earth in comparison to you? Naught!
17. Without you, I can't find my way. Please never leave. Please never stray.
18. Now I know what it means to be truly loved. You take good care of me.
19. I know I'm supposed to take care of you, but the truth is, I absolutely love doing it!
20. You did your best, and that matters. I love you!

21. I have the best company in the world. You!
22. Our love is undefined!
23. My arms can't wrap around you tight enough.
24. The path of my life led me to you, and I have no regrets.
25. As long as we're together, life can take its time.
26. What is the word FUN without U. Absolutely no fun at all!
27. We're like notes on a keyboard that play the most delightful sound.
28. I treasure you.
29. No chart or stick can measure our love.
30. Our love is the most perfect song.
31. Every time I hear your voice, I feel so safe, loved, and secure. So calm and so mellow, without choice, it leaves my heart assured.
32. You are not "tolerated." You are deeply loved.
33. Beloved, you're a blessing to me, EVERY DAY!
34. I'm smiling ear to ear. You did that!
35. Our love connection is just so natural and right.
36. You for me = a wonderful blessing.
37. We're not as cute apart as we are together.
38. I love you, and you love me. How much better can things get?
39. Me, I love. You, I love. But the two of us together…I love, love!
40. I found you, you're mine. That's it!
41. I'm not a gambler, but I'd bet on us any day of the week.
42. Days, weeks, months, years. What's time when I'm with you?
43. We're my favorite.
44. Our love is a nice, warm fuzzy.
45. Love…know this…I'm rooting for you.
46. We have a lifetime to peel all the layers of us. Let's just take our time, sweet love.

47. If I'm the question, you're the answer.
48. Let's sail this ship and make waves.
49. There are red flags of warning and white flags of surrender. No red flags here, babe. I surrender!
50. If no one has told you, understand that no one has to, because I'll always tell you. Sweetheart… you're perfect!
51. Our relationship…I'm all in!
52. If I'm the chimney, you're the fire.
53. You…me…There's only one way this can go. OUR way!
54. Like the ripples of waves at sea, softly, gently, flowing free. Where er' you are, I'd love to be, for you were fashioned just for me!
55. Yes, I'm looking. You shouldn't look so fine!
56. I thank your mom every day for having you just for me!
57. My love language is YOU!
58. When you get home, it's never soon enough. I missed you like yesterday!
59. All that I was void of, ended when I met you.
60. Life may be a rollercoaster, but we'll just buckle up and laugh and scream together. Let's go!
61. I love you on Monday. I love you on Tuesday. I love you on Wednesday, Thursday, Friday, Saturday, Sunday, and any other day they may invent.
62. I love how you patiently wait for me when I'm not ready on time, but I don't want to take it for granted. Thank you, sweet love.
63. I love how you support me even when you're not sure my ideas will work. You're so dear to me.
64. I love how you hold my hand when we are out in public. It makes me feel like I'm 16 again.
65. The encouragement you give me brings me back to life and gives me the strength to fly!

66. Our time together means more than I have words to say.
67. You're very, very, very, very, very, very good to me. Very!
68. Stay forever. Please?
69. Don't forget sweetheart, please come back, because I miss you already.
70. Moments with you can't be calculated with time because time doesn't exist in our lovely space.
71. Lying next to you is like sweet flowing waters; calm, cool, and serene.
72. I love the way you express your feelings. It lets me know you feel comfortable with me.
73. I don't consider our silence awkward. I could stare at you all day and never say a word.
74. Don't worry. I'm sticking around, forever.
75. The moment I locked eyes with you, the rest of the world disappeared.
76. You bring life and health to my soul, and sweet joy to my heart.
77. Who better to experience life with than you? No one. Just my opinion.
78. I'm so glad you looked beyond my surface and really saw me!
79. We just mesh, and I love our mesh because it's just that: OUR mesh!
80. You're my warm blanket when I'm cold, and even when I'm not.
81. Every day we'll never end. Every day begins again. Come on, love, let's get started.
82. We're doing this together. That's it.
83. The right place at the right time, and here we are, babe. I love you.
84. We just vibe, and I'm lovin' it!
85. Let's travel to the moon and never come back!
86. Our love is a song with the perfect tune.
87. We're just good together.
88. We work, and that's enough.
89. What is love without us?

90. My life was meaningless until the day you walked into it.
91. You are so patient with me, and I want you to know I'm extremely grateful to have you in my life. Thank you so much, honey.
92. I love how you rub your fingers through my hair while you talk to me. It reminds me that you care.
93. You're never a maybe. You're always a yes!
94. Whenever you feel in doubt about my love for you, just take note that I'm still here and remember I said, "I do."
95. Let's take that leap and ride the clouds forever.
96. You're extraordinary to say the least, so give YOURSELF a hand.
97. My space + you = EVERYTHING!
98. You're my Sundae on a Sunday
99. Guess I'm stuck with you. Yay! That's fantastic!
100. YOU'RE the reason the sun comes up.
101. You illuminate the room with your smile. You're like daylight.
102. Our love is like the fragrance of a sweet perfume.
103. Since the day we took that leap, your heart I will forever keep.
104. You, next to me, is everything!
105. Your touch refreshes my soul.
106. You're the only regift I ever want.
107. There's no better way than to start my day waking up to your perfect face.
108. You deserve far better than me! Thanks for choosing me anyway. I'm so honored.
109. Why would I want to take the highway when I can take the slow scenic route with you?
110. I don't.... I don't mind saying "I DO" again and again and again!
111. When others say words that hurt, you bring life to my bones.

112. Your ability to take care of my needs, even though you have little time, speaks volumes!
113. Understand this: You are MORE than enough for me!
114. When I think of the love we have between us, I can't help but get emotional.
115. What would my life be without you in it? I don't want to know.
116. I'm pinching myself because it's hard to believe this love we have is real.
117. This we have…I love it!
118. Every time I have to leave your presence, my heart breaks.
119. Our "happy ending" is just our beginning. Let's get started again, babe.
120. I love you on purpose. I promise.
121. My life plan changed when I met you, and you were definitely worth it!
122. You're still a yes, for me.
123. All guards are down, my heart is open, but only for you, my love.
124. May our hearts dance together forever.
125. I love getting to know you more and more each day. You have so many layers, and I love the revelation of YOU!
126. Everything I desired and asked for, God gave me wrapped in you.
127. The more I get to know you, the more intrigued I am to know you more.
128. You're my human sofa. I'm so comfortable around you.
129. I love just watching your lips move while you talk. Keep talking.
130. Being with you is like Christmas every day. And Valentine's Day too!
131. I love how intentional you are with me. It means the WORLD to me. Just want you to know, I see you.
132. You're the best thing that happened to me since Jesus.
133. You make my hard days tranquil and serene.

134. I love being around you. You're fun, loving, and you fill all my once-empty spaces.

135. God heard my prayer and answered it with you.

136. You are WAY above what I prayed for.

137. I love how you rub your hand around my neck and shoulders when I'm feeling stressed. It brings me so much comfort. Thank you so much, my sweet honey love.

138. You amaze me when you bounce back as if you never had a hard day in your life.

139. Every time I think I've figured you out, you yet amaze me!

140. You make age want to redefine itself.

141. I'm always here to lift you when the world lets you down.

142. Your embrace feels so divine.

143. Come love, let me whisper sweet "somethings" in your ear.

144. I get you, and I'm here for you. Always!

145. You're not difficult, you're just you, and I love you just the way you are!

146. I value your opinion simply because I value you! You are so important to me.

147. If good looks are against the law, then sweetheart, you are under arrest.

148. I love how you compliment me when I dress up. It makes me feel confident. You're my beloved.

149. I'm always here when you're ready to talk. My ears are all yours!

150. You amaze me with how talented you are. There's so much to you!

151. Me + You = too much love in the room.

152. My heart turns to jelly whenever you're near me.

153. I love love, and I love, love you!

154. Is there enough paper in the world to write what you mean to me? The answer is a resounding NO!

155. Forever starts over every day I'm in your presence, and that's a beautiful thing.

156. I still can't believe we happened. I'm so happy!

157. There's only one you, and you're all mine. Lucky me, lucky me, lucky me.

158. I didn't know life could be so beautiful and wonderful and sweet, and fun until I met you, sweet love.

159. With you in my life, I win every time.

160. I love how you smile when you look at me. It makes me feel desired.

161. You're still so youthful and bright. You're just so amazing!

162. Every time you walk in the room, the atmosphere changes for the better. You bring serenity into my space.

163. Come, sit next to me so my space can be happy.

164. Our time together seems timeless.

165. What's missing in my life, just walked in the room.

166. I'm not confused. I'm mesmerized!

167. I never have to feel like I'm falling, knowing you're my net of support. I appreciate you more than words can EVER say!

168. It's cruise control with you, babe. No need to hurry when I'm spending time with you.

169. If I seem like I can't stop smiling, just know it's YOUR fault!

170. You make my world feel like spring even when it's cold outside. I'm so blessed that you're mine. I love you so much!

171. I'll always believe in you. When others think you'll never succeed, I see your potential.

172. Is it possible for two people to love each other as much as we love each other?
173. You're my very own book of poetry.
174. In my arms, you can rest from all your worries. It's okay, babe.
175. Breathe. I've got you.
176. You make my heart pitter-patter, pitter-patter, pitter-patter.
177. With you, every passing day gets sweeter
178. You have awakened every cell in my being and brought me to health. Yes, just your being in my life did that.
179. You don't need the key to my heart. I left it unlocked just for you.
180. The more I get to know you, the more I understand true love.
181. You're perfectly perfect but just for me.
182. You're faithfully lovely. How can that be?
183. You're my comfort when the world is uncertain.
184. I love the way you handle me with so much care and intention. It's appreciated.
185. I'll always be here to help you bounce back when the world beats you down.
186. It's like the sun makes its entrance when you walk into the room. Everything changes for the better.
187. Whatever your plans are, understand they are now my plans too.
188. The conversations, laughter, and all the good times, money can NEVER buy.
189. Fantasies are one thing, reality is another, but you're both to me.
190. Let's play this love story by ear. We can't go wrong.
191. Your smile makes me smile.
192. You don't have to do a thing, and I'm still impressed.

193. You… It's a yes for me!
194. You're my favorite, hands down.
195. This love story is continued til forever.
196. I've achieved my top goal. You!
197. I love how you take time out of your busy day just to spend time with me.
198. The word amazing doesn't begin to describe you, babe.
199. Apart from you, I'm lost.
200. Since the day I met you, my feet have never touched the ground.
201. Into my life, I'm glad you came. You're a priceless work of art in a frame.
202. You're not just a "looker," you take my breath away!
203. Because you're here, I'm staying.
204. I'm so glad I chose you, but more than that, I'm so very grateful YOU chose ME!
205. One day, you walked into my life. Today we're here, FOREVER!
206. This love of ours is no fairytale. It's purposeful and a very intentional reality yet to be written.
207. The small things you do are HUGE!
208. Special moments make for special memories, all with special you! And that's very special!
209. I feel the warmth of your love, even when you're nowhere near me.
210. You're not just a breath of fresh air, you're a wind of fresh air.
211. I love that you love me, but more than that, I love HOW you love me.
212. The moment I saw you for the first time, that was it!
213. I love you. I LOVE you. I love YOU!
214. You're proof God far exceeds what we ask for.
215. My mind is made up. My heart is fixed. It's you now. It's you forever!
216. You share your love so generously, but I won't lie, I want it all to myself.

217. I can't believe this isn't a dream; you're here in my presence.
218. I'm glad I never allowed you to cross my path. I grabbed you first.
219. After all this time, I'm still excited about you.
220. When it comes to you, call me a gatekeeper.
221. I can't live without you. I can't live without you. I can't live without you!
222. You're just for me. Wow! Lucky me!
223. Your presence soothes all my aches and pains. I am well because of you!
224. Our problems are temporary, but this love … it's forever!
225. You are the embodiment of perfection!
226. I love how you hold my hand when I ride with you in the car. It reactivates the sparks we had for each other when we first met. Thanks, honey!
227. It's your fault I'm so happy.
228. You're the secret I can't keep.
229. I'm staring because my eyes are stuck on you.
230. Being with you is ALWAYS a plus!
231. The next time you decide to look so good, warn me so I can get something for the butterflies in my stomach.
232. Out of all the dears, you're the dearest!
233. I asked for a kiss and got sugar! Lucky me.
234. You add spice to my bland life.
235. The mold God made you from is so precious, He wouldn't dare break it. Are you kidding me?
236. I'm undeniably blessed. How so? Because you chose me!
237. Sugar and spice don't make EVERYTHING nice. But YOU do!
238. I'll always be your steady, for you have always been mine.

239. I love how you are always there to wipe the tears from my eyes when I can't hold them back.
240. "Love is not proud or rude." You are kind and humble. I appreciate it more than you know. Thank you, sweetheart!
241. I wear your love like it's a coat. It brings me so much warmth.
242. You're like a rare jewel on display, untouchable, secure, and priceless!
243. Time will age us, and that's okay. Just know I'll love you anyway.
244. You're clearly a gift from God!
245. I'm grateful for the lavishment of your love.
246. "Love is patient and kind." Thank you for being patient. Thank you for being kind.
247. Faithful, I'll be to you till I depart this life. I promise. Still.
248. Your sweet words are not just flattering to me; they uplift my soul.
249. When I'm discouraged, you encourage me, and that changes everything. I didn't know I could fly! Thank you, love.
250. The sound of your voice settles all my anxieties.
251. Let's put one foot in front of the other and start this life together, my sweet love.
252. "Love is not self-seeking." Thanks for all the times you thought of me, and did for me above yourself.
253. I'll always be by your side. It's ride or die!
254. I love how you say one hundred sweet words without saying anything at all.
255. I can't wait till you get home. Anticipation…
256. On a scale from 1 to 10, you're a 2… 2 fine to be measured.
257. "Love is not easily angered and does not keep record." Thank you for being truly forgiving.

258. I'll always be your earthly peace in the midst of your storm. Rest in my arms, sweet love.
259. I can't wait to retell this beautiful love story of ours one day. Until then, let's continue.
260. I choose you today, tomorrow, and always. Read this again tomorrow.
261. Understand this: You're only second to God, my dear.
262. You're not anything. You're not everything. You're not a thing at all. You're mine's and that's a special thing.
263. I'm always grateful I said, "I do," and even today, I still say, "I do!"
264. I love how you tend to me when I'm not feeling my best. It means the world to me. Thanks, honey.
265. "Love is not envious or boastful." Thank you for your humbleness, love. I notice.
266. Grow with me, love. Flow with me, love. Let's do this thing together.
267. When I was void and empty, you came into my life and made all the difference.
268. Sweetheart, your words bring life to my bones and courage to my heart. I can do this!
269. I love how you smile at me even when I'm not looking my best.
270. Some days, I feel incapable of giving you the love you deserve for loving me the way you do, but I promise to do the best I can.
271. You stole something from me. It was my heart.
272. My rescue plan is: run to you.
273. I'll spare not one good thing from you, my sweet love. Not one!
274. I love how you cheer me on when I'm trying to make money moves. What a great support you are, my love.
275. I promise to always make our house feel like home. Get comfortable.

276. “Love rejoices in truth.” Thank you for always being honest with me, even when it's uncomfortable.
277. Whether on the mountain top or in the valley, our love will always remain.
278. Our love shines. We can’t help it, and we won’t try.
279. This is OUR love thing. We do it OUR way.
280. Stand with me on the frontline of our love, and we’ll always win!
281. I’m grateful I saved myself for you and thank you for saving yourself for me. I feel special.
282. “Love perseveres.” Whatever we go through in life, we’ll do it together. We’ll NEVER give up. Period.
283. I’ll defend our love at all costs. We’re in this fight together!
284. If you win, we won!
285. Your love for me makes me want to stand on the rooftop and tell the world!
286. You’ve always been so loyal and kind, and I just want you to know that I’m grateful for that.
287. This has been such a joyous union, even through all the ups and downs of life. Lets continue this dance together.
288. You are kind, respectful, and full of love. Today, I honor you.
289. Let’s take this love all the way to the finish line together!
290. Together. That’s the secret of our love.
291. Here we go. Together!
292. “Love protects.” Thank you for always protecting me to the best of your ability. It makes me feel so safe.
293. I delight in making you happy! Come, my love. What do you desire?
294. I can’t always read your thoughts, but believe me when I say, I feel you.

295. Together, there is nothing we can't accomplish; there is nothing we can't overcome, there is nothing we can't win. Together!
296. When you hurt, I'm here with arms open wide. Come, love, come.
297. I love you all the time. When in doubt, remember that, sweet love.
298. "Love hopes all things." With you by my side, I'll never give up!
299. Come, let me hold you like it's our last night on earth.
300. You're an unwritten song playing over and over again in my heart.
301. Hearing our voice heals my soul.
302. I trust YOU with my HEART, my SECRETS, my SPACE, and my TIME, and you can trust ME with YOUR heart, YOUR secrets, YOUR space, and YOUR time.
303. I'm not the best with words, so I hope my actions show how much I love you. I'm trying.
304. Your kiss changes my whole day for the better.
305. Loving you has taught me what enduring love means.
306. "Love trust." It means the world to me that you trust me. I pray never to take it for granted.
307. Even on the days that we feel disconnected, I still choose YOU.
308. I know you work long and hard days and sometimes don't feel appreciated. Just know when you get home, you will be!
309. I was yours yesterday, and you were mine. I am yours today, and you are mine.
310. Still me, still you, we're stuck with each other like glue.
311. Being with you reminds me that love is still alive.
312. From the time I wake up till the time I go to bed, I can't stop thinking about you.
313. Thank you for making me laugh. It makes me feel young and free again.

314. “Love never fails.” When I feel like giving up, your love always lifts me. Thank you, babe.
315. There is no love like our love because it’s OUR love!
316. I haven’t forgotten I said, “I do.” And I still do!
317. If you fall apart, don’t worry, I have glue.
318. If I could live inside of you, I still wouldn’t be close enough. But I’ll keep trying.
319. You’re beyond perfection. Is there a word for that?
320. Come, love. Let us unveil the many levels of our love, again and again.
321. I’m liking, I’m following, and I’m subscribing.
322. How much do I love thee? I can’t count the ways.
323. Before I could ask, God answered with you.
324. You far exceeded what I had asked for.
325. I’ll bet on you every time.
326. Apart from you, I’m lost.
327. One life on this beautiful earth, and I am so blessed to spend it with you.
328. I’ll withhold no good thing from MY good thing, for as long as I breathe.
329. Let's take a stroll hand in hand, down uncharted territory, and leave our footprints in the sand.
330. When I’m with you, I feel like I’m on a secluded island, just me and you.
331. Like!
332. Our relationship is already next level, so it can still only get better.
333. I don’t mind sharing personal space but only with you, love.
334. I’m going to have to wear shades because every time you walk in the room, the sun follows.
335. The song of you keeps me dancing. You’re my endless love.
336. You revived me from a lonely place. I am fulfilled.

337.When I’m awake, I think about you. When I’m asleep, I dream about you. You’re ALWAYS on my mind.

338. Sweetheart, I'm mad! But not at you. ABOUT you!

339. And they lived happily ever after. WE are they.

340. Once upon a time ended up being forever! I’m so glad I said “I do.”

341. This fire shall never be extinguished.

342. Remarkable is just the lighter side of you.

343. All things wonderful wrapped up in you! You’re the perfect gift, love.

344. You’re the only member of my membership-only club.

345. It’s simple… I love you.

346. You’re an earthly taste of heaven. I love you, Honey.

347. The love you show me gives me the assurance I need to let my guard down. My heart is yours, my love.

348. This we have…Yes and Amen!

349. Let's ride on the waves of the wind together and see where it will take us. Ready?

On the following pages, the Love Notes may be considered gender specific.

Female to Male

350. Because you care for me so tenderly, I feel safe.
351. I love how you pamper me for no reason at all. You're the sweetest ever!
352. I can't wait to rest my head on your chest.
353. Your eyes pierce my soul like a sunray on an array of gemstones.
354. You're dashingly debonair!
355. I can't wait to hold that charmingly dashing physique of yours.
356. Being with you reminds me that chivalry still exists. You're such a gentleman.
357. Brains, check. Braun, check. Charm, check.
358. I love how you wrap your arms around me and let me cry in your chest when I'm overwhelmed with grief. You're so loving and kind.
359. The word handsome doesn't begin to describe you.
360. I see you, my handsome love! Read this again tomorrow.
361. Intelligence and charm in the same package. Wow!
362. You are a gift wrapped in a suit.
363. I'll never see you the same because you just get more handsome by the day.
364. You know you're my favorite guy, right?
365. I'll never see you the same because you just get more handsome by the day. I love how you'd rather spend time with me than hang out with the guys.
366. Sweetheart, you're not just handsome, you're fine! And I'm head over heels in love with you!
367. You can't help that you were born so handsome.
368. Your good looks are mesmerizing.
369. You're flawed. You're imperfect. But that's what makes you so attractive, and perfectly so.

Male to Female

370. Sweet darling, I'm overwhelmed by your beauty!
371. Were you born looking so gorgeous?
372. I love how you cater to me after a long, hard day. It makes me feel respected and appreciated. Thanks, beautiful.
373. Give me your worries, sweet love. Rest.
374. I can't wait to caress that voluptuous silhouette of yours. Hurry.
375. You're captivatingly stunning!
376. Your eyes sparkle like precious jewels in the sun.
377. I can't wait to rest my head on your soft, subtle breast.
378. Ravishing you are my love. Ravishing you are.
379. Can there be a painting as beautiful as the one standing in front of me?
380. Beauty, check. Brains, check. Personality, check.
381. The words to define your beauty don't exist.
382. I see you, my beautiful woman. Read this again tomorrow.
383. Wow! Stunning and smart in the same body.
384. Blame yourself for the smell of roses in the room.
385. Your beauty leaves me without proper words.
386. You are the Earth's most beautiful fragrant flower.
387. With you, every passing day gets sweeter.
388. You're a gift wrapped in a dress.
389. You know you're my girl, right?
390. I love how you wrap your arms around me and let me cry in your breast when I'm overwhelmed with grief. You're so compassionate, my love.
391. Your beauty is incomprehensible!
392. What flower are you today? A rose? Gardenia? Bird of Prey? No, my sweet love. You're the whole bouquet!

393. Sweetheart, you're not just beautiful, you're absolutely gorgeous, and I'm head over heels in love with you!
394. You prove that beauty is more than skin deep.
395. Who made you so beautiful?
396. I love how you'd rather spend time with me than hang out with your girlfriends. You're so selfless.
397. When I got you, I plucked the most beautiful flower.
398. Beauty doesn't define you. You define beauty.
399. The sparkle in your eyes brings warmth to my soul. You Radiate.
400. Every imperfection and every flaw is what makes you so beautiful.

About the Author

Robin B. Roundtree is an Evangelist, Creative Freelancer, and entrepreneur born and raised in Wichita, Kansas. For nearly 25 years, she has devoted her life to ministry, using her gifts to uplift and empower those who are often overlooked. As the founder of *Project: Can Anything Good Come from the Hood*, inspired by John 1:46, Robin has created meaningful opportunities for individuals to showcase their talents through expressive arts such as skits, praise dance, and singing.

Guided by unwavering faith and supported by her loving family, Robin continues to serve as both hands and feet in the mission field. Her heart for people leads her into the highways and hedges, meeting needs where the harvest is plentiful but the laborers are few. Through every endeavor, she remains committed to inspiring hope, nurturing purpose, and shining light into the lives of others.

www.ingramcontent.com/pod-product-compliance
Lightning Source LLC
LaVergne TN
LVHW070202110826
845147LV00002B/478

9781967603060